KT-529-101

Little Cow

Jan Barger

Belitha Press

LIBRARY SUPPORT FOR SCHOOLS
VICTORIA BUILDINGS
QUEEN STREET
FALKIRK
FK2 7AF

Mama Cow and Little Cow were resting in the afternoon sun.

...eturned on or before
...stamped...

Little Cow

First published in the UK in 1998 by
Belitha Press Limited, London House,
Great Eastern Wharf, Parkgate Road,
London SW11 4NQ.

This edition first published in 1999

Copyright © Belitha Press Limited 1998
Illustrations copyright © Jan Barger 1998

Jan Barger asserts her moral right to be identified
as the author of this work.

All rights reserved. No part of this book may be
reproduced or utilized in any form or by any means, electronic
or mechanical, including photocopying, recording or by any
information storage and retrieval system, without permission
in writing from the publisher, except by a reviewer who may
quote brief passages in a review.

ISBN 1 85561 862 1 (paperback)
ISBN 1 85561 801 X (hardback)

British Library Cataloguing in Publication Data
for this book is available from the British Library

Printed in China

Editor: Honor Head
Designer: Helen James
Calligraphy: Jan Barger

'Move, Cow!' said the farmer.
'I can't get my tractor past you.'

'Moo,' said Mama.
'Little Cow is sleeping.'

'Move, Cow!' said Horse.
'You're in the way.'

'Moo,' said Mama.
'Little Cow is sleeping.'

'Move, Cow!' said Donkey. 'I've got to meet some children for a ride.'

'Moo,' said Mama.
'Little Cow is sleeping.'

'Move, Cow!' said Pig.
'I want to get to my mud puddle.'

'Moo,' said Mama.
'Little Cow is sleeping.'

'Move, Cow!' said Sheep.
'I need to find my flock.

'Moo,' said Mama.
'Little Cow is sleeping.'

'Move, Cow!' said Tortoise.
'I'm in a hurry.'

'Moo,' said Mama.
'Little Cow is sleeping.'

'Move, Cow!' said Hen.
'My chicks have scattered.'

'Moo,' said Mama.
'Little Cow is sleeping.'

'Please move, Cow,' said the
farmer's wife. 'It's feeding time.'

So Mama Cow took Little Cow
home for supper.

LIBRARY SUPPORT FOR SCHOOLS
VICTORIA BUILDINGS
QUEEN STREET
FALKIRK
FK2 7AF